TINY TREE
CHILDREN'S BOOKS

First Published 2019
Tiny Tree Children's Books (an imprint of Matthew James Publishing Ltd)
Unit 46, Goyt Mill
Marple
Stockport
SK6 7HX

www.tinytreebooks.com

ISBN: 978-1-910265-70-3

© Andy Rigden & Jim Landen

Happy reading,

Lan Yvet
Lauren.

Andy and Oli

For Sarah, and our monsters,
Harry and Maddy

For Bella, Alf, Joe, Poppy and Sid.

My mum's a bug-eyed monster,
With a bug-eyed monster's head.
It's bigger than a pumpkin
And it's really rather red.

My mum's a bug-eyed monster,
With arms that reach her knees.
She's wider than a wardrobe
And can pull up tiny trees.

Some mums are small and dainty.
Some mums – tall and elegant.
My mum stomps around the house
Like a baby elephant!

When we go out shopping,
People turn their heads and stare.
They snigger at Mum's curly tail
And giggle at her hair.

Sometimes this would annoy me,
Sometimes it made me mad,
That people gawp at monsters
And think all monsters bad.

But I was never that upset,
Until Harvey came to tea.
My mum was wearing face cream,
She was quite a sight to see.

But what made Harvey jump,
What caused him most surprise,
Were the large cucumber slices
That were covering Mum's eyes.

Harvey was still shaking
When he went home to bed,
And though Mum looked fine again
Thoughts raced around my head.

If Mum made Harvey shake,
And he saw her every week,
When it came to Sports Day,
Would my whole class shriek?

That night I lay awake
And worried in my bed.
I imagined the reaction
To my mum's bug-eyed monster head.

I imagined my friends fainting.
I saw some mums turn and flee.
I pictured my class teacher,
Hiding half-way up a tree.

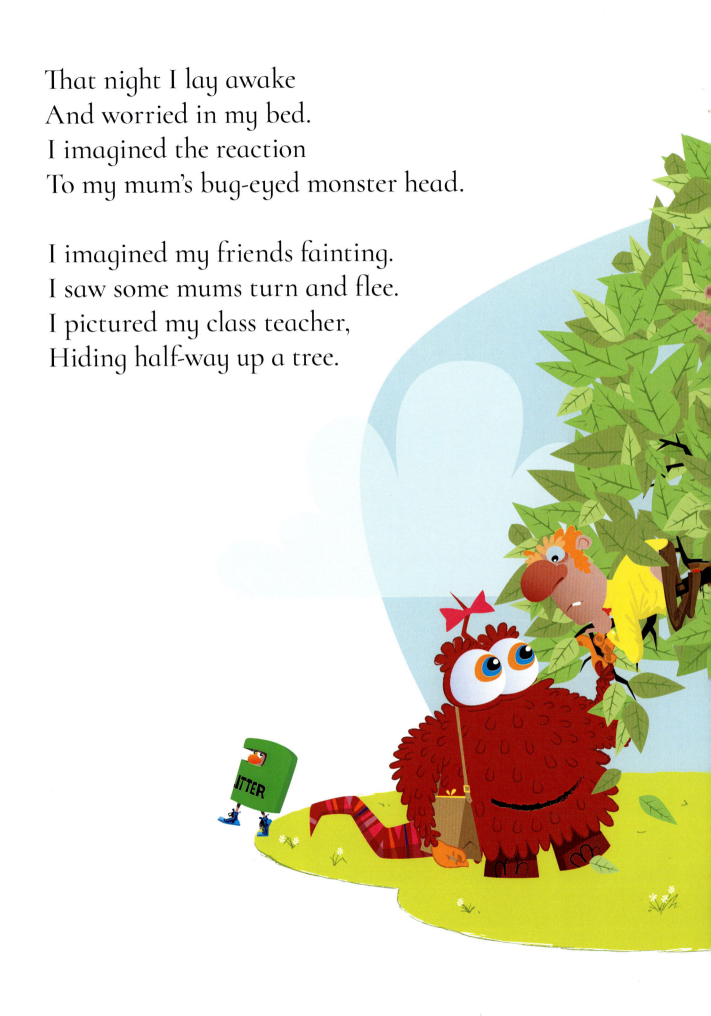

So when the big day came,
My heart was beating like a drum.
When Mum and I walked into school
My legs were wobbly and numb.

But I had no need to fret,
I had nothing much to fear.
No one fainted when they saw us
No one turned to stare and leer.

My mum was in the best of form,
She had all the mums entranced.
She told them funny stories
And did a little dance.

But it was when the races started
That my mum would steal the show.
She sparkled in the egg and spoon
And dazzled in the wellie throw.

When it comes to wellie throwing
The champion mum was Cilla's
(But a lovely throwing action
Can't beat arms like a gorilla's.)

My mum broke all the records
On her very first attempt.
And when she took a second turn
No one saw how far it..............

"LOL!"

went.

My mum's a bug-eyed monster,
But she can lob a wellie.
Her final throw went so far
It featured on the telly.

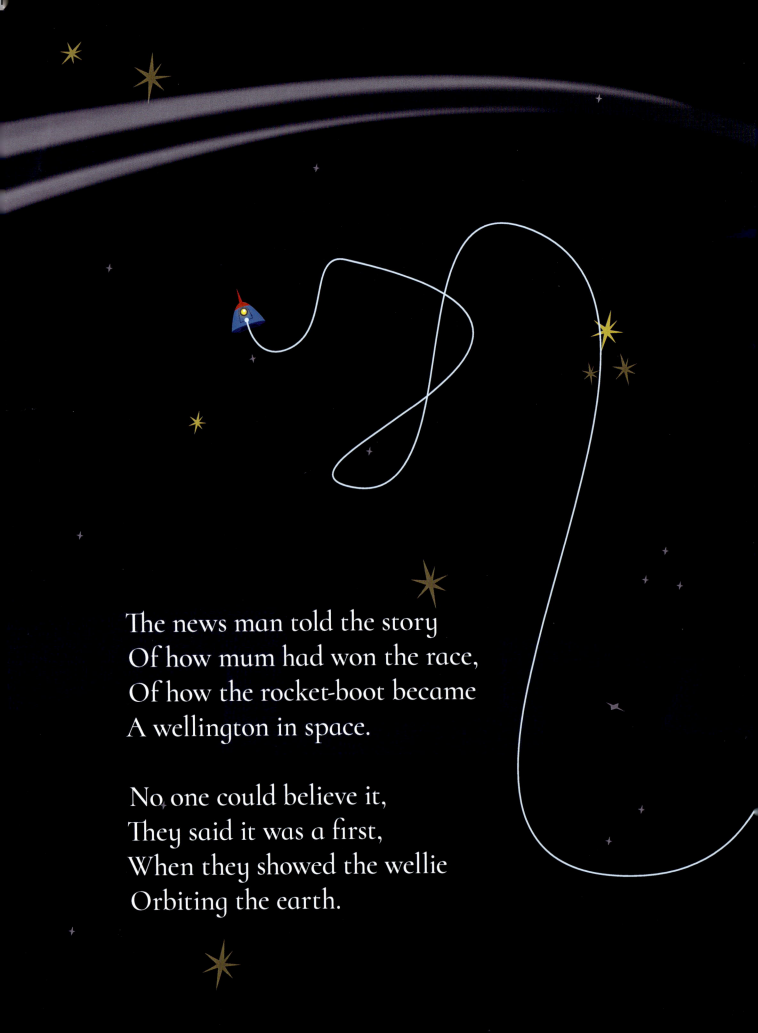

The news man told the story
Of how mum had won the race,
Of how the rocket-boot became
A wellington in space.

No one could believe it,
They said it was a first,
When they showed the wellie
Orbiting the earth.

When I went to school next day
I was the centre of attention.
The races and the wellie throw
Were all my friends could mention.

"I'd like a mum like yours,"
 My friend Harvey said.
"I'd like a monster for a mum
 With cucumber on her head."

I said, "I'm sorry Harvey,
I know this will be a blow,
But my mum is not for sharing
And there's something you should know:"

"My mum's a bug-eyed monster,
 She's a monster through and through.
 But that's just fine with me,
 Because I'm a monster, too."